Won't Change His Spots

My friends said:

'You clever clogs.'
Carmen.

'Total rubbish.'
Henry.

'Interesting.'
John.

'Is this one of yours? You should get it published.'
Ged.

'Loved your poems.'
Celia.

'The nature poet of Whitstable.'
Fiona.

'You're really good.'
Clare.

Won't Change His Spots

An anthology of fiction and poetry

Sally Turner

ISBN: 9798309108787
First edition
Copyright © 2025 Sally Turner
All rights reserved.

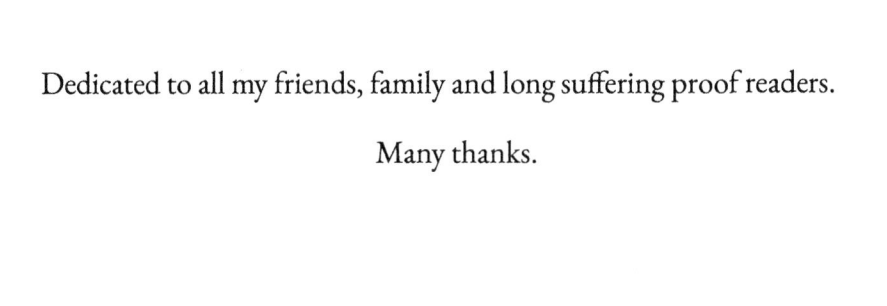

Dedicated to all my friends, family and long suffering proof readers.

Many thanks.

Contents

To the mortar board...............9
Winter Musings....................10
Won't Change His Spots......12
Secret History.......................29
Spring Offensive (or Not My Gardener).............................30
You won't believe what happened to me today..........32
Rhapsody..............................34
Uncle Freddie.......................35
Memoir of a School Girl......44
Little Brother.......................50
Soil..53
Over the Dead Body............54
Fire starter again...................58
Out on the Red Sea. Day One 64
Breaking out.........................65
Empty Nest..........................66
Humidity..............................67
For Jacki: who died March 2024....................................68
To Gerard.............................69
To make an apple crumble...70
Garden: New Amsterdam. Surinam................................71
Marooned............................72
Two Beds.............................76
Acknowledgments...............79

To the mortar board

No, actually,
You are wrong.
I'm not another, 'Brick in the wall.'
I'm so much more than fiery baked clay
Held with mortar and straightened with a plumb line.
On a summer's day I glow
Reddish hues in sun light
Form intricate arches
And bear the weight of years.
I can be moss covered and ivy hidden
Form the base of a canal
Bring a lifetimes' work to a steel furnace
And yet bake your bread.
I have strength in numbers
But alone can be a murderer,
Build you a castle or a station,
Hold water for your ducts
And stands for your car.
Made by an Indian woman
A Roman slave, sold by the ton
Counted on by millions.
Why should I be humble?
I am Brick.

Winter Musings

When I wear white socks
The dirt is always black. But
On black socks, it's white.

Planting tulip bulbs
Too shallow, will feed squirrels
Not my crystal vase.

Washing my windows
Gives seagulls a chance to aim:
Guano splattered glass.

Wearing a white shirt
And eating tomato soup
Creates polka dots.

The ink runs out as
I write a special line for
My friend's birthday card.

Just before a fall
My brain says, 'Be careful now'
And then I tip up.

The candle wick burns
Faster than the yellow wax
Yet floats in its pool.

There are mince pies still
In the freezer. Will they last
Til next year's party?

Insufficient sun
For solar lights to work so:
Night gardens stay dark.

Frost on the scaffold:
Roofer climbs with care and tools
Face taut with deep thought.

Cold outside, warm room
Steamed up glasses, foggy view:
The blurred book titles.

Some seeds need cold to
Thrive. In spring they will burst forth
And carpet the earth.

Won't Change His Spots

With his smile carved into his face, Ring Master looked down into a basket full of half cubs. Hybrids. Leopards. Crossed. A mixed bundle. Spotted. Clambering. Nuzzling. Padding and patting. Alert and careful. Feline. Killers. Sharp claws and kitten teeth. Mewling and baby babbling.

'I want this one,' Ring Master, grasped the alpha male by the scruff of the neck.

'He's special, alright. Do you proud for sure.' The leather aproned woman busied herself with illicit pedigree documents, a vaccination certificate, tagging information and the paper receipt for an eye watering sum of money that changed hands in the shadows.

'He will be called Leopold,' he told her. 'Add that to his documents.' He placed Leopold into a large soft leather bag which he slung over his shoulder. 'Nice doing business with you.' He tipped his black hat in her general direction.

That was the day Ring Master became a single parent.

He was an invested parent. He always checked the bath water temperature with an elbow. Leopold always screeched. As was natural. Ring Master used the fire guard assiduously. Leopold was protected. He explained to turn the toaster off at the wall before inserting a knife to free a bulging crumpet. Leopold knew butter was generously supplied.

Ring Master was never cruel or overly harsh. He believed that to get the best results one had to show love and kindness. A turned back or a truncated stroke of the ears he found was more effective than a whistling whip or the slap of a paddle. His very high standards were shared in stages always appropriate to Leopold's developing skills.

'Crouch like this,' he demonstrated. 'Head up, now,' he cooed.

Leopold was content. His fur was sleek and his body, lean. As the weeks and months passed his strength developed. Long in the thigh, he could leap fearlessly; holding his high domed head with pride. He was a little stubborn. Which cat is not? He asked careful questions,

'What's for tea?'

'Are you my dad?'

'Can you do this?' as he executed an almost vertical take-off.

Ring Master smiled indulgently. Smoothed back Leopold's ears. Whispered that he loved him.

Patiently Ring Master introduced Leopold to the life of the circus. A gentle training regime. A familiarity with following instructions. A deal of praise when Leopold was successful. Leopold was successful.

Most evenings, Ring Master spoke of the performance he expected Leopold would enact. Leopold lazing by an open fire, fur almost smouldering, Ring Master coaxing and wheedling. Leopold listening intently with the embers reflecting in his eyes. Ring Master insinuated ideas. Dripped his plans. Introduced the concept into the training programme.

'We could try a higher stool. Eh Leopold? You are getting tall now.'

'Try clawing the air with your front paws. What would that look like? Oh, well done Leopold. That is very good.'

Leopold was game. His natural inclination and intuition was excited. He would leap from stool to stool and through rings. He was rewarded well. Nepeta and cat mint. A rare chocolate.

One dusky evening they sat chatting, 'There must be peril,' mused Ring Master. 'All circus acts have peril. You have seen the high wire?'

'Yes, I've noticed there is no net. If the high wire walker wobbles and falls it's enough to break bones.' Leopold knew his own skills lay elsewhere. Ring Master had told him.

'And the galloping horses and bare back riders?'

Leopold agreed he had seen the potential danger of being stampeded over, crushed by flailing hooves.

'The jugglers face enormous risk too. You have seen them in practice?'

'Yes, I agree that tossing knives and swords is a dangerous act. But what is it you want from me?' he asked. Inside, he already knew.

'I am alone with you in the cage,' said Ring Master. ' You are stronger. You are faster and more lethal than me. I am defenceless if you turn on me. What protection do I have except a flimsy wooden stool?

There is peril in all that for me. Hopefully, only perceived peril.' He added with a smile, 'But Leopold, there must be peril for you too.'

Fire, thought Leopold. You want fire. The element I should fear and cower from. Flames: too close I scorch and burn. My fur will be ash. My whiskers will shrivel. My tongue will blacken. My eyes blinded.

'Do you really want that?' Leopold asked.

Ring Master stopped stroking his fur. His voice hardened. 'I cannot force you. But I can teach you how to face that peril and make it something magnificent.' His voice became liquid again. 'You have to trust me Leopold. You are no good to me if you are hurt. It is not the way we do things here. A spark not a flame. Protection and perfection.'

'Easy words for you. My peril will be real. Yours imaginary.' Leopold growled deep in his throat. Ring Master believed he was purring.

Cautiously, the new training regime began. Ring Master used precise timing: tapping his cane as the flames cooled round the ring. The air was rank with paraffin fumes. The floor covered in wet sawdust. The spectacle was of Leopold flying through a ring of fire. It was a frightening and stunning performance.

'A few minor theatricals could be thrown in,' said Ring Master. 'A bit of snarling and reticence or even disobedience might look quite good for the audience. What do you think?'

'I think I should tear your head off, but I won't,' said Leopold. 'Oh, but I could... 'Partner',' said his interior voice.

ooo

Always the swaying cages, the fumes from the diesel engines and the crunch of gears as the trucks hauling the trailers laboured over the mountains. For some, the straw was little protection against the biting wind and the cruel flurry of snow, cold on the tongue.

Invariably it was a night journey to the next stop. A late evening of hurried, shouting breaking of camp. A constant urging to go faster, pushing and pulling, folding the Big Top canvas and clanging of chains. There was the roaring and chipping of sweating bodies, too closely confined. The sulphurous lash of the whip as it uncoiled and then snapped. There was the knowledge that no matter how experienced they might be, movement of the troupe was always a shock. For some there would always be containment. For some there would always be the inevitable isolation.

Leopold was the star of the show. Top of the bill. In a firmament of his own. His aloof demeanour was partly from feline haughtiness, partly from circumstance, partly because he had no other place to be. He had no choice. He could pace. He could turn from his metal metaphorical bars. He could sprawl in the straw or lie in a trailer. He was the entertainer, a professional. He had standards and a position to keep. But there was always tension.

The circuit of venues grew each year. The demands of the crowds ever more hungry for daring, excitement, originality. The clowns now juggled with chain saws on the backs of roaring motor bikes. The trapeze artists ever higher, had no nets, no wires. There was fear and laughter and wonder from the crowd at the magic of balance, control and speed. There were months of rehearsal and practice and risk. Timings gone wrong and injuries disguised.

And Leopold, leopard man, trained and lithe.

ooo

Each evening at seven o'clock, the lights in the Big Top would dim. Then a clanging noise and a cool breeze would flow into the tent as the massive internal cage was swiftly erected within the arena and saw dust scattered afresh. Pure theatrics. The crowd seeming to be protected from the danger of the act to follow. The stink of paraffin as the first of the massive rings was fired. The spot lights searching the cage to find Leopold on his high stool. Wrapped in his blue and gold cape. Snarling. His teeth bared.

He would paw the air and the lights would glint from his glittering claws. The children of the front row would hide their eyes behind their hands or seek the reassuring arm of a nearby parent.

Then hush.

The red coated Ring Master. A round man with a black hat and a cane under his arm worn as a swagger stick would enter the caged arena. Alone. Unprotected. Could he make the leopard man jump from his place of safety through the ring of fire? Fire. A natural enemy and anathema to the leopard. But often a friend to man.

Still hush.

A baby's crying stifled. The ring burning a dirty yellow. Gesticulation from the Ring Master in the arena. Would Leopold jump through the ring or attack the red coated man?

Leopold considers this option every time he is faced with the fire. Maul or singe? Risk a tail shortened, or a bullet for an attack? Lose a whisker at a misjudgment or a life? One of nine.

If he makes it, the next ring in the show will be smaller. The ring after that, smaller still. A three ring circus act. He will always burn.

There is the crackle of the flame and the flame reflected in Leopold's eyes. In the stillness of the Big Top the only movement is the flicker of the flames and Leopold as he gathers his muscles for the launch. A quiet word and he leaps. He closes his eyes to protect them. He wills himself a rocket. He clears the ring and the crowd breathes in and then out, and all is noise.

He circles the cage growling at the crowd as agreed. He is all pent-up anger and disgust at their need for a thrill. Two rings to go. He returns to his high stool and combs his whiskers. Seemingly unconcerned as the second ring replaces the dud and is fired. Ring Master struts into the spotlight to explain how much smaller is this ring. 'Ladies and gentlemen, boys and girls,' how much more dangerous for Leopold.

Leopold knows it. In practice and training he can clear it easily. But in practice and training it is not always lit. Leopold needs to appear magnificent and proud not cowed and smutty with soot. His spots are not scorched onto his fur. He never wants them to be.

Leopold lands clear and the crowd screams their appreciation. He tosses his head with pride as he circles Ring Master. He makes a feint in his direction and Ring Master backs away, apparently worried. Is this an act? He brings his cane forward and 'reestablishes' his authority. Leopold returns to his stool, satisfied he has exerted some of his own power. No one in the crowd could hear their exchange. 'One more ring. You are an arrow. You know the centre. You can triumph.'

'Damn you.'

Ferrara. The place to build a reputation for fearlessness, ruthlessness. The venue for the greatest acts on Earth. The crowd knowledgeable of circus skills when circus troupes pass through yearly. Leopold's act of leaping through the smallest ring of fire unscathed is renown. His life devoted to its success. Or lose it.

He turns his back on the flaming ring. He gazes into the crowd. He sees the excitement and fear on the faces of the audience. Their expectation palpable. They will his success. But they do not want it to come too easily. His tail sways behind him. He makes his voice gruff as he growls low in his throat.

'You want more?' he asks of them.

Ring Master taps on the cage bar gently. Leopold turns his head but not his body. If he jumps it will be when he wants to. Ring Master could command. Ring Master could demand but in the end it is Leopold who is the star. These people have come to see him. Chain saws are all well and good. Prancing red nosed baggy trousered frolicking fools entertain the children. Here he is. Let him savour this moment before the inevitable.

He turns, measures and leaps. His whiskers ash at the tip from a spark. His tail brushes the deepest yellow coolest flame. The water douses the heat. The ovation is overwhelming.

'Remember, Ferrara. There will be nothing greater.'

Now dressed in his mighty blue and gold swirling cape, the leopard man disappears into his trailer.

ooo

The tedium. The training. Night after night the performance. The applause. The fitful sleep. The uncomfortable barracks. The loneliness. The yearning for some companionship of his own kind. A year or two of being at the height. At the prime. As the most revered and most wanted. Could his luck last forever? Could the skill remain honed? Leopold was no fool.

Each morning as he stretched, he felt the slightest tightness in his muscles. It took him just a little longer to ease the ache out of his hamstrings. He stood as tall and strong as ever but deep down he knew that age does wither and no amount of training and wishful thinking could capture that instinctive spring or avidity of eye.

Ring Master was as relentless as ever. Leopold was his classiest act. The draw. What the audience demanded. He had no substitute. So many circuses piled up the human pyramids to the struts of the tent, the strong men, circus parents, balancing their children at the top.

The furthest to fall. The lightest to carry. The easiest to toss. Only he had Leopold. Alpha. Unique.

Their dates in London on the South Bank had been long booked. A residence in the gardens near the County Hall. Come one, come all. A magical time of awe and wonder promised. Posters plastered around each train and Tube station. A ticket booth in Leicester Square for one of ten intriguing circus experiences. Nine nights. One matinee.

Injuries to circus performers are not uncommon. Sprains, broken bones and bruises are usual. Being bitten and kicked are occupational hazards to all. Losing a finger or an eye can be calamitous and career ending, depending on the career. Being bullied, groomed, harassed and starved into submission, a dirty secret. All possible. All feasible. Leopold had seen it all, experienced some and was fearful of others.

Nine standing ovations had swelled and echoed over the South Bank. Commuters late in Waterloo Station had heard the roar and shared their train with the twittering audiences heading homeward with tired children and boisterous friends. 'Amazing. So glad you suggested it.' 'What a show!' 'Did you get that photo at the last ring?' 'Incredible!' 'Never seen anything like it.' 'Almost freakish!'

In his trailer, Leopold was tired. A day of rest ahead. Some stretching exercises before the last show. Some good food. A few words with Ring Master. Not necessarily in that order. Some sleep. No one knocked on his trailer door to congratulate him or to invite him to join them for some down time. It was ever so. Late that night they would strike camp and head for the Winter Fair in Berlin. But first was the finale of their London residence.

As the sun slowly warmed the mist from the Thames, the circus troupe were up and limbering for their last show.

The big tent filled. The acts perfected, performed. The drum rolled for the final act. Leopold was ready.

Two rings successfully navigated.

Later, as he lay in the antiseptic sheets, salved and bandaged, he tried to explain what had gone wrong.

'I misjudged it by a whisker. I was blinded by a flashgun from the audience. I clipped the edge of the ring. That's why it fell'. A pause. 'Will someone please tell me how bad this is?' He moved a bandaged limb.

'Not to worry now, Leo,' soothed Ring Master. He was shaken too. The opening in Berlin was only three nights away and his best act was now unlikely to be there. 'The burns are more than superficial. But you will heal. You need to rest and recuperate and relax. You have worked so hard.'

There was a very long sigh from Ring Master. ' We have to move on but there will always be a place for you if you want it.' He moved his hand away from Leopold's arm. 'When you have recovered, I will be in touch. Do not think I will forget you.'

Ring Master slipped away leaving Leopold swathed in white linen, corpse like. It pained him to move physically. But his mind was racing.

ooo

Years of rich cooking odours had seeped into the plaster work and steam had coloured the ceiling yellow and caused darker blotches. The white ceramic tiles were clean but chipped and the work surfaces were rubbed raw in places. The doors of the cupboards didn't close quite vertically nor the drawers horizontally. An old champagne cork had been used to prop the washing machine level. On the window sill, cat mint in a pot and bright red fiery birds' eye chillies bloomed.

Leopold an early riser, was still in his leather slippers with his silk dressing gown tied neatly at the waist. Vibrating air from the heated kettle caught the light as he reached above it for his chocolate, cup, sugar and milk, lifted deftly from the fridge. He moved with his customary fluency and grace. The leanness of his outstretched arm belying the hidden strength in his sinuous muscles. He made his chocolate quietly, comfortable now in his solitude, perched on the high stool of his kitchen.

He put aside his paper, having routinely scanned the headlines, arson being his least favourite news item, and pulled open a corner cupboard door. He lifted gingerly, from the lower level, a large rectangular metal box and hoisted it onto the table. It was dark green and grey with a rusted looped catch and two rusting hinges. The top was dented with a shape like paw prints and the label smudged and illegible. Leopold opened it with care and affection. He rummaged around its memories and contents, withdrawing out a familiar and loved few and placed them deliberately next to each other on the surface. One of glass, one of wool, a relic from a younger more innocent age, one of linen. He breathed the Nepeta from the little linen bag deeply.

Leopold patted his dressing gown pockets and found his glasses. His flat padded fingers touched each piece delicately. He gently toyed with the marbled glass ball enjoying the way the light refracted from it making sparks and splinters. He made the beams dance across the back of his paw and bounce from the walls. His eyes, with the vertical iris of the marble, bright behind his spectacles, watched avidly.

He started. The doorbell rang again. With reluctance he replaced the objects in the box and clipped the catch before, with all his litheness, he ran down the uncarpeted stairs. He had lived long enough to use the caution of the city dweller. He paused and placed his eye to the spy hole. Who he saw filled him with rage.

There could be no pretending to be out. If he could hear the breathing of the unwelcome visitor, surely he could be heard too. He paced a little, feeling caged.

Leopold opened the door unwillingly. The man on the doorstep was, in contrast to Leopold, rounded and he wore clothing for the weather: an old-fashioned black hat and a cutaway red coat. He carried an antique cane.

'I wasn't expecting to see you,' growled Leopold, pulling the belt around his waist a little tighter. It was a reflexive action.

'Obviously...but surely, Leopold, we should let bygones be bygones? Are you going to invite me in? Darn chilly on the doorstep.'

'You could at least tell me the nature of your visit.' Leopold's voice kept its gruff edge. He didn't want this man in his house. It was his space and he felt protective of it and the independence it afforded him.

'In good time...' Ring Master was over the threshold, in the hall, his foot on the stair. He raised his face expectantly. 'Having chocolate, are you? I wouldn't mind a cup.'

Leopold sulked behind him. 'In the kitchen, have a seat. I'll make you one. Then you can tell me how you found me and what you want.'

'Still got that old box I see. Places that has been eh? It is one of the things I always associate with you, Leopold, that and the smell it has.'

Leopold felt his hackles rise. 'Don't touch.' He moved it to the side away from the Ring Master's prying fingers. Could nothing be his own? 'Here's your cup. Perhaps now you'll tell me...' He crossed his arms and ankles as he stood with his back to the window and leaned on the sink. He looked carefully into Ring Master's face, trying to read him.

Inside, Leopold was fuming. The last time they had been together had been a less than happy occasion. He didn't want the memory of that disturbing the calm world he had created for himself now. He stroked his ear. Unfortunately, just the sight of the hat and cane had been enough to start the internal churn.

'Well. finding you was not difficult. A few discrete enquiries, a few bundle of notes. You know how it is. You are still rather a novelty after all.'

Ring Master sipped his hot chocolate. He studied Leopold over the rim of the mug. Leopold looked back, unblinking at the man who had brought him up, loved him, supported him and then, gone.

'I have a proposal for you.' Ring Master leaned forward. He sat on the high stool awkwardly with his feet pointed backwards under him. He was sweet and sticky like a lollipop on a stick. He took another sip of the chocolate. 'It will mean some good money for you and looking at the state of this place, I do not mean to be rude Leopold, a lick of paint would not do much harm would it? You could afford to have it done out and still have enough left for...'

'I like it like this.' Leopold glanced out of the window and watched the sparrows on the roof of the house opposite fluff and dodge. He could feel an involuntary twitch of his face. He flexed his pads instinctively.

'Leopold. Le-o. I know things were hard for you. But we had our good times, too? Remember Ferrara, how exciting it was. The applause. The ovations. You were the best. Top of the bill. I will go as far as to say you were mag-nif-icent.' Even now, he couldn't resist a touch of the theatrical.

One whisker twitched. Leopold wanted to be unmoved.

Ring Master changed tack. His voice was lighter. 'The troupe miss you too. We were a good team, most of the time. Anyway,' his voice hardened just a little, 'we need you. We need your class and your agility. Without you, I hate to say it, it is not working. It is too tame. The crowds are not coming. I think you owe us one more time.'

Leopold bristled. 'I owe you? What do I owe you? Didn't I do enough before? I made your reputation.' His voice tightened. 'Weren't the risks I took every night sufficient for you? It wasn't you, was it? You were all safe down there. It was me. Time and again. And I'm the one who got burned. Keep your dangerous acts and your money. I don't want any part of it. You've had enough of my lives.'

Leopold flexed. He remembered the camaraderie of the group and his isolation from them as the 'star'. As the leopard man. One of a kind.

'As for the others,' he continued, 'let them make up their own minds. But I doubt they'll want to face all that again. They saw what happened. I listened to you too many times. You made me listen, now I don't have to listen any more.' He turned to dismissive him.

'So,' the man laid expansive square hands on the table. 'You are sure? I can't change your mind? That stubborn streak in you was always in the way.' He drummed his fingers and Leopold turned and couldn't help but follow their movements with his eyes. The man leaned back a little and cast a crafty look at Leopold.

'I will tell you what. I will cut you in fifty percent of the box office.' His fingers tapped each point for emphasis. 'That will be more than generous and I have regard for your risk and expertise. Leopold you were bred for this...'

'No! I've heard enough of your wheedling and cajoling. I didn't want it before and I don't want it now.' He searched for the perfect steel in his voice and found it. 'There are some things that can't be changed. My scarred past, my mind, my...Leave. Now.'

The man sighed. He pushed his cup away and stood up heavily. He was so much shorter that Leopold. Yet he had once had so much power and influence over him. There had been a time when he had told Leopold to leap, and he leapt. Leopold would leap through fire for Ring Master. Not again.

'Well, thanks for the chocolate. Don't worry. I'll see myself down.' Ring Master stopped at the top of the stairs. 'Oh, nice addition. I had not noticed that on the way up. Three rings...very clever.' Ring Master leaned closer to read the etched inscription in the bronze. 'Claus of Innsbruck. I have not heard of him. But nice piece," He tapped the wall with his cane. It was a noise that made Leopold flinch.

His clipped footsteps faded down the staircase and the door closed quietly. He left behind the faintest whiff of sulphur and a sprinkle of sawdust.

Secret History

Punk.
I was punk.
My hair was leopard spotted
My boyfriend was an addict.
I pierced body parts
Wore safety pins
Shouted truth to power.

Now Polystyrene
Is a quiz answer
And Siouxsie Sioux
An eyeliner shade.
Discordant sounds are sampled
And there is no SEX
On the Kings Road.

Are the DIY knitters
Repair cafes
And guerilla gardeners
My rebirth of Punk?
I still say,
'God save the...'
With a snarl.

Spring Offensive (or Not My Gardener)

Buzz saws
Magpies soar
The ride on lawn mower roars
It's the death of the daisies.

Weeds are in the barrow
The borders edged and narrow
Straight as an arrow
With bedded Marigolds.

He slides the slick from off his tines
He doesn't hear the Mandrake's cries
The sweet peas are tightly tied
He makes the willow, upskirted, weep.

But chain sawn hedges sprout,
And cherry blossom petals flout
His watered lawn in the drought:
It's the battle for neat and tidy.

He ranks the tulips like a boss
Uses a flame thrower on the moss
Bent double he plucks out dross:
The eyes of dandelions.

He'd change the sod
The wooden logs
And ponds for frogs
For acrylic blooms in pink.

But his dreams are racked
With bramble bracts
Tall nettle traps
And Bella Donna's berries.

The weeds invade
His plastic glades
And Nature rises up again
His regiment defeated.

You won't believe what happened to me today…

I was spewed.
A million like me.
Surrounded with cloudy cool chaos.
Gradually conglomerating into speckled jelly.
Hanging by the side of the pool.
Pushed by the ripples.
Slimy and shiny.
Bobbing. Refracting the light of day.

Of what do I dream during the balmy Spring nights
when the moon glows on the water?
My chia seed body to grow big and strong.
My energy to multiply each cell.
I'm deeply still but inside I'm bursting with
minute movement.

For days I quiver.
Imperceptibly my shape transforms.
I elongate so slowly.
Translucent tail.
A flick of life…
My wriggling disturbs the unctuous home I share.
We are yet contained, restrained.

The rain is deafening on the water.
Each drop bangs onto the water lilly leaf
under which I cower.
When the shower is over, I feel refreshed and new.
I have woken to find another part of me.
I can stretch and flex.
I'm on my way.

I leave behind the egg white
mass.
I can see the green edge of the
algae
and can nibble at its fruits.
I grow rounder, stouter, thicker,
longer.
Stronger.
My textured skin develops a
greener tinge.
I am a symphony of curved
and glistening shapes.
I look into the world
with horizontal eyes
and see the dancers on the water
who will dance for me.
 All is solid.
I have leapt from my globular
safety.
The marsh grass is dry. For the
first time I am alone
And then I hear that voice.
Deeply sonorous.
Resonant.
It's mine.
I'm calling.
I'm shouting out the glory
of what happened to me
Today.

Rhapsody

Blue blood in my veins:
Look!
The blue in my iris:
See!
The blue rinse in my hair:
Washed out!
My blue stockings:
On the line!
The ink dry:
The Tat is private!
My very language:
WTF!
Be very glad
I don't sing the Blues.

Uncle Freddie

'So, at this point, that would be Uncle Freddie.'

My Mum and I are sitting at her dining room table holding pencils. She's tapping with hers. In front of us is a piece of wall paper, lining paper to be accurate, curling at the edges and weighted down at the corners with mismatched saucers, liberated from the garage. We're sketching a family tree. Of sorts. I'm trying to help Mum remember the names of our relatives before her memory fades away and all I'm left with is a pile of black and white photographs, with no idea of who they are pictures of, or just the title of their relationship to her or me. Great Great Grandfather. Great Aunt.

Until recently, I had been content not know their names in full. But there was a programme on television called 'Heir Hunters' and a few days previously I had received a phone call from them asking if the name 'Slater' meant anything to me. I thought it was a hoax. It was not. Despite my complete need to inherit a fortune or even half of one, I had to admit that the name did not ring any bells. But as I've already said, I operated at the level of 'Great Aunt Sissy.' I had no idea of her full name. She was long dead. Her name might have been Cecilia Slater. The only person I had contact with who might know full names was my Mum and so the conversation about who was who on our family tree.

'Right. So, if that branch contains Freddie, did he have any brothers and sisters? Did he get married? Did he have kids?'

I could see Mum conjuring up the vision of the man and struggling. Was he her uncle or great uncle? I'd never met him. He was high above me on the branches. Was there a photograph of him in the shoe boxes she kept full of Kodak papers, loose negative strips and the lock of hair in a small brown envelope? Apparently not. There was a photograph of a striking looking young man in a striped pullover called Johnny. They hadn't married but despite the years my Mum still got a dreamy eye and a pink cheek at the mention of his name. Johnny Bates. Not a relative.

'Mum?'

'Yes, I'm thinking. What do I know about Freddie? Well, I'm going out for a cigarette. You make us a cup of tea and we'll go on in a bit.'

She padded off to the 'smoking room'. In reality, the garage, where she sat on an old chair, wrapped in an old purple anorak, her feet on a roll of moth-eaten carpet to keep her feet off the cold concrete floor, surrounded by the flotsam of worn-out domestic appliances and the 'could always come in useful someday' objets d'art or something like that. She came back reeking of Peter Stuyvesant Lights and sat back at the table.

Big pause. Sip of tea.

'I remember something about Freddie. He did do something of note. I can't remember what you want, like a name, but he did do something.'

Pause and sip.

'He painted a picture. A portrait of a young man. It was very good I'm told and it was put on the wall in the Birmingham Museum. It was on display for a long time. We used to go and look at it.'

'Did I see it? Did you take me?'

'No.'

'Is it still there? Oh, why not? What happened to it? What happened to Freddie?'

'I don't know. All lost in the mists of time. I expect it was put in storage. Thrown out in the refurb. The painting, not Freddie.'

'Good joke, Mum. Drawing a blank then? Geddit?'

'Do you want to carry on and try a different branch?' She was obviously not that amused.

* * *

When I got back to my house a few days later, I had the rolled-up lining paper and a few more names filled in on the tree. My Mum had found a Slater but obviously not the one from whom I was going to inherit my vast fortune. My interest was piqued by the idea of the portrait done by my relative. A picture good enough to be framed and hung in a museum with a label and everything, for the public to walk past or stop and look at. I wondered who was in the picture. Was it a self portrait or a model? I had a lot of questions and no answers easily available.

Looking at the family tree we had created I wondered if there were enough clues to track down the elusive artist. After all, the Internet was invented for such armchair sleuthing. Also, my neighbour was heavily into, nay, addicted to 'Genealogy Is Us' and possibly he would lend me a hand to get started. For a small fee. A cup of coffee anyway.

That's where I started. A rolled-up piece of lining paper, a latte and a password to a database of a million, million souls and secrets. Waiting to whisper to me.

Piecemeal. Dead ends. Typing errors. Registers only partly retrieved. Sore eyes. Genuine lack of patience. 'Pay if you want to see more.' Public records now privately owned. Nebulous. Monetised. I raged against Somerset House and the need to pay to find Uncle Freddie. I stared out of the window to collect my thoughts. Refocused my eyes on distant trees before plunging back in and trying a different route through the morass of the relevant and irrelevant. Armchair sleuthing was not proving to be quite as straight forward as storytellers would lead you to believe.

Around four o'clock my neighbour rang my doorbell. He was wearing at least three jumpers, a sure sign he had been online in his cold study. He had fingerless gloves too and the end of his nose was pink. Another indication of his addiction to 'Genealogy Is Us.'

'Hi. How are you getting on? Any break through with the uncle yet?'

'No, not really. Are you coming in for coffee?'

'Yeah, OK. I might have something to tell you.'

He doesn't really have a sense of humour or if he does, he doesn't share mine. He's always serious and kind of straight. That probably makes him a good researcher.

Once seated in my kitchen he said,

'I approached it obliquely. I couldn't resist a bit of a dabble. So based on what you'd said I think I've found a name, a date of birth and you, my dear, might be going to the ball after all.'

This was most unlike him to use any form of metaphorical language in my hearing in all the years he had lived next door.

'I'll put it simply. I tracked cousins up and down the tree and I found Frederick Slater.'

'You're joking!'

'No. I don't think I am. I think this is the one you are looking for.'

He sometimes does use 'Star Wars' echoes.

'Anyway, I called up Birmingham Museum and spoke to some bloke who is a curator and he looks after the archive. Did you know only a tiny fraction of Birmingham's art collection is on show? They have vast cellars full of stuff they haven't sold off yet. Well. To the point. There are some pictures or portraits, whatever, in the archive. They're stored as canvases, maybe cracked and dirty, I don't know. Not popular now, kind of out of fashion but in his day this Slater was well thought of.'

I was rapt. My Mum had been right.

He continued,

'So, I foraged around to see if I could find out any more about Frederick Slater and found his Will on line. Small price to pay. I got to read it. His money, estate and so on was left to the remainder of the Slater family.'

'Goodness, you've done a lot better than me. I suppose the next step will be to try and track down some more contemporary Slaters. I wonder if that is what 'Heir Hunters were doing? Looking for people with connections. No obvious heirs. Maybe you could get a job working for them.' I wasn't joking.

* * *

Like Tess of the D'Urbervilles I'm claiming kin. I'm not above the odd literary allusion myself. Some phone calls and a DNA test confirmed that we were beneficiaries of the Slater estate. It turned out to be a mouldy old cottage not a million miles from Kinver Edge where we used to go on caravan holidays when we were kids. What a very small world. Mum was both shocked and excited that a strange quirk of family births, marriages and deaths had brought us here.

The cottage was sitting; well listing slightly, in an overgrown garden and had boarded up windows to the front. The key had been handed to me by a sandy haired solicitor in his sandy coloured office off Colmore Row. With a twist and a shove we were soon standing in the motes of the dusty hallway and I was wiping strands of web off my face. No electricity of course and it was very cold.

'Do you think Uncle Freddie lived here?' I wondered.

'I have no idea. But no one does now, and not for some time by the look of things. Piles of circulars behind the open front door. It smells of damp.'

My Mum could always be relied on to smell damp. Her memory was occasionally fuzzy but there was not much wrong with her legs or her determination to poke about.

'It's yours and mine,' she reminded me. 'Come on. let's have a jolly good look - drawers and down the back of the sofas.'

'You've been watching too many cosy crime capers in the afternoons, Mum. Anyway. what do you think you, sorry, we are looking for?'

'Dunno. Something interesting.' She wandered off into the once living room, now a grimy shell filled with overstuffed chairs and very faded chintz. Not much taste in furniture, I thought, for an artist. But then who knew who else had lived here with and after Freddie.

I don't know what I was expecting to find. A black velvet bag of uncut diamonds or a desiccated mouse; some glued together Christmas decorations or a hoard of gold doubloons; a painting of exceptional quality hanging in plain sight worthy of a Sotheby's auction or a cushion stuffed with...

Mum had emptied the contents of the dresser drawer onto a chair and was sifting. Her attention was complete. Proper archaeology.

'I'm going upstairs to see if there's anything in the attic room.' I said.

It had been a man's room. The telltale sign was a mirror hanging just too high over a chest of drawers and a certain austerity to the place. There was nothing obvious to say Uncle Freddie had been an inhabitant. No brushes easel or tubes of paint, half squashed. It felt a bit strange to call him Uncle Freddie. He wasn't my uncle. But no matter. There were three drawers and a small wardrobe to look through.

Maybe, it was an inherited trait. On the top shelf of the wardrobe was a shoe box. There were no shoes in it. Like my Mum's habit it was crammed with black and white photographs, yellow at the edges, a little box, some certificates and a couple of letters still folded into envelopes. I took it downstairs.

'Found anything, Mum?'

'Not much. A lot of dust and a tube of hand cream. It's getting too dark in here to see clearly now. Let's bugger off and get some tea. We can come back tomorrow with torches and bags.'

'I'm bringing this box with. We can look through it at yours.'

We drove for a few minutes and then I asked. 'What do you think?'

'I think it's derelict and needs pulling down'

'No, I mean do you think we might find something? Clues about Frederick Slater?'

'That box of goodies you've got might proffer a solution to the mystery,' she replied, channelling her inner Miss Marple. Really? Proffer?

We spent the better part of the evening poring over photographs of complete strangers who meant nothing to us and had little if no family likenesses. There were some inspiring clothes. It was the little box that contained the secret of Uncle Freddie. Nestled in its navy blue felt interior was a lapel pin, inscribed. Amongst the papers a letter of commendation.

Uncle Freddie, once famous portrait painter and distant relative of mine turned out to have been in the Secret Service. The name was Slater, Frederick Slater. Commended for bravery for being a spy. A Secret Slater.

We had another cup of tea and a fig roll each.

Memoir of a School Girl

School Winter Uniform 1967

Box pleats.
They're wide
They're corn flower blue
They form a skirt that droops
To the knee.
Every other skirt is straight:
Two inches shorter
Two inches longer.
Buy mine at Rackhams
Designer floor for uniforms.
Designed to keep us safe -
But rolled around the pudgy waist
Times five -
A flare of stocking tops...

* * *

The local girls' grammar school had a bad reputation. All the girls were highly visible to my god mother who with pursed lips, explained that they smoked cigarettes openly while still in their uniforms when they walked past her house and they were loud. Almost criminal. The school I was sent to was two long bus journeys away. No one knew if the girls there were loud and smoked after school. It was a wealthy area and it was thought that the locals would attend. Mainly, they didn't. There were as many riff raff there as in my local area. The irony was not lost on me.

I was in the B stream and we didn't mix with the A stream. They were an elitist bunch of stuck-up prigs and that was on a nice day. We looked down on the C stream who were a bunch of pitiable thickies. Gold, silver, bronze was never so fiercely instituted. Most of my early life there I fought to get into the A stream but was never promoted despite my grades being better than the lower levels of the A stream. 'Better to be top than middle'. It still rankles. I hated them and wanted to be in the elite corps.

Life was made tolerable because I had a friend. Maguerita Carmen. Musician, language expert, long dark pigtails, a cross-body purse, she wore a satchel on her back and an attitude of total bravado. She had a single parent family like mine, free school lunches and a love of reading horror stories and satanic verses. She knew a lot of swear words, didn't do her homework, and could play energetic games with competence.

I hated hockey where you left the muddy field with battered shins and swollen ankles; netball where your face was mashed by a large leather ball; tennis where you spent fifty minutes picking the ball out of the net because Mary Barnet had a private tennis coach at her club and could serve properly, and cross country was for dodging behind the bushes for a Number 6 cigarette or whatever brand had been filched from an unsuspecting parent. I liked swimming, alone.

Miss Morant farted in P.E. when she demonstrated leaping over the 'horse'. I couldn't stand up. Nor could I hit a ball with any kind of stick, baton, racket if you had begged me to.

* * *

The School Gym

It's cold light and airy
Purpose built and ugly
Snaking ropes tamed on the walls.
Today is 'teams'.
I stand in line
My yellow aertex shirt is tight
My breasts bludgeoned overnight
Arms folded
Squashing, not disguising.
Shorts reveal the white legs
Of holidays in wet Welsh caravans.

Caroline is Captain
She's always captain
She likes sports
She has straight blond hair.
She picks her team.
The line dwindles
I'm not the last one chosen.
(We know who that will be)

I'm not last in the pecking order.
I'm tall and useful in defence.
But that doesn't stop
The feeling of being
The after thought.

* * *

Like Carmen, I too, had eaten dog biscuits. We caught the same bus home some of the way, and I was happy to be a ' partner in crime'. I believe it was curiosity not evilness that caused our reputation. At lunch we spent time in the Biology Prep. room next to Mrs. Mould the senior lab. technician. You couldn't make up that name. She was a great companion for seven years. Young, beautiful, perfect make up, and a degree, she knew all the sciences. Carmen and I loved being there.

It wasn't our fault that the locusts swarmed and escaped when we lifted the lid of their glass case to get a better look; that the frogs escaped from their glass case when we lifted the lid to get a better look; that the book we prized had the pages glued together as we lifted it gingerly out of its glass case. Obviously to get a better look. We were so sorry. We loved Biology. It was about us, our world, our feelings for nature all rolled together with the blackberry picking, the workings of the inner ear and the blur of field trips to cold streams to find creepy crawlies and count them. We relished a coach trip to strange parts away from our suburban landscape where we had to sleep on lumpy horsehair mattresses in bunk bed dormitories where we stayed awake all night telling stories.

I didn't understand it then, but I was taught by a number of blue stocking women who had lost beloved ones in the war or perhaps didn't have one, and they found solace in female company. They gave each other lifts home; they lived together; they arrived in the morning in their own bright red sports cars.

Some of my younger teachers had been to Warwick University and had Germaine Greer lecturing them in English and politics. My teachers taught me modern poetry and feminist theory all rolled together. They were an eclectic mix of personality and style and joy. I didn't fall asleep in their lessons. Carmen and I translated Chaucer together, agreed and argued about Ted Hughes, Eliot and Tennyson.

* * *

Warrior of Shalott

She left the web, she left the loom
She made three paces thro' the room
She saw the water lily bloom
She saw the helmet and the plume
'I'm half sick of shadows,' she cried
'I feel completely dissatisfied.

No silly curse shall hold me back
That useless weaving is old hat
No fading in my silent tower
Cometh the woman, cometh the hour.

My face is fair, my blood is hot
I have no need of Lancelot
He can hum his tuneless song
Waiting is the greatest wrong.

I have a sword and armour bright
Like all the knights I'm off to fight.
I'm not bound by this tight girdle
Towards my destiny I hurtle.

On burnished hooves my war horse trots
Towards the towers of Camelot
To defend the castle and the keep
And so all enemies to defeat.

And so my name thro' out the land
Will echo for my brave last stand
No image in a mirror bright
I will own my name in lights…
'The Lady of Shalott."

(With thanks to Tennyson).

Little Brother

When you have a little brother, you'll always be the elder. With being older comes massive responsibility. 'He's so much younger than you.' 'Remember, he's younger than you.' 'He broke it because he didn't know better.' 'He's still a baby.'

It means that you, by every measure, must be different. More grown up, not a baby, able to know better. And so, where to begin? With Teddy? The fire? The dead body incident? Each one of these stories involves me being the grown up. He was left in my unwilling care and he played the role of the child. We were fifteen months apart in age.

Let's start with the Teddy story. It was a childhood's summer's day. Always a blue sky and a garden to play in. A long-suffering dog was dressed up in left over baby clothes and was panting in a pram while being pushed around by a very bossy mother. Another child was playing quietly in another area and having the usual babble conversation with a soft toy. What was Little Brother doing? Having covered Teddy in soil he decided that Teddy needed a wash. The most easily available water at that moment was from the Kitchen down pipe as real mother emptied the sink of tea leaves, oily gravy and Fairy Liquid. Poor Teddy did not come clean.

'You should have watched him more carefully.' 'Teddy is ruined now.' 'Maybe Little Brother will grow up to be a plumber.'
Is it giving the game away too early to say that he did? Well, a gas fitter.

Our school summer holidays meant long tracts of time left to our own devices. We made up our adventure stories and activities. We were bored yet inventive.

We moved house every three years or so and this new house had a very long garden that ended at a metal railing that separated the garden from the railway embankment. The last quarter was wild and overgrown and this was the patch of land that was turned over to us to play in. I decided we should dig to Australia. Little Brother was too young to know how far that was, but I knew it was far away and to get there we would have to divert around the hot centre of the Earth. It was going to take us some time. We had a fork, trowel, spade and all summer.

Each day we donned our wellies, took up our tools and marched to the pit. Each day we laboured in the hot sun, the pit getting wider, not deeper. We had hit the clay substrate and without a pick axe, we couldn't break through. Some blistered hands later, it became sadly obvious that Australia was just a dream. A new game was needed.

A children's television programme we had seen demonstrated how a magnifying glass could focus the light from the sun onto paper and make it smoulder. We both wore glasses. We were both long sighted so our lenses were like magnifying lenses. We wondered if dry grass could replace paper. What a brilliant idea! We had a safe place to try it out as our pit was about four feet in circumference and far enough away from the edge we felt there could be little chance of a fire spreading. Little Brother pulled a handful of dry grass and put it in the middle of our pit.

With scientific concentration, born of seven years of experimenting with eating coal, licking blood from scratches, watching worms disappear, I focused the lens and within a minute there was a lick of flame. I stamped on it. Flushed with success and full of ambition, Little Brother pulled a bigger pile of dry grass to make a bigger flame. Pyromania is very exciting. We both stamped on the flames.

Then a tiny little breeze came up and a tiny bit of a smouldering blade of grass was whisked into the surrounding tinder dry, drought dry, tall stemmed grasses and within seconds we had a burning inferno to one side of us. There was heat and smoke. I told Little Brother to run to the house and get Mum while I tried stamping on what I could. He ran away on podgy legs. 'Get Mummy. Fire.' I could hear his mantra. 'Tell her to bring water,' I yelled.

She arrived with half a bucket. The rest had splodged out as she followed Little Brother towards the smoke. I was looking in fascination at a man with a jacket in one hand and a briefcase in the other who was flailing at the wall of yellow flames which were fast spreading over towards the railway embankment and our neighbour's garden. Little Brother started to cry and Mum seeing the seriousness of the danger rushed back to the house to call 999.

The fire brigade arrived. The fire was quenched. The man with the singed jacket was gratefully thanked. The Firemen were flirted with.

'What were you thinking of?' was asked of me. I was seven. I obviously wanted to set the world alight. But more of that later.

When Little Brother started his own business as a gas fitter he called it Firestarters.

Soil

We were kids,
We played in the dirt,
Mud pies.
We ate the dirt,
We planted stuff in the dirt:
twigs and grass seed.
We threw the dirt at each other,
We dug in the dirt on our way to
Australia.
We hid our dirty secrets under
the dirt.
We lied about our lost dolls and
then
The dirty sheets, our dirty
underclothes
Our guilty pleasures.

Dirt is good. Dirt is soil.
Dirt under the fingernails
A gardener's hand roughened by
the dirt.
Not a farm
Not an allotment
Some patio pots crammed with
tomato plants.
Dirt is the shit of worms,
Of micro stuff and bacteria
goodness
Of fungi magic and stars.
It doesn't look like star dust
But it is.

Over the Dead Body

30 August 1972.

My diary entry:

Went to Amroth Beach. Swam in the sea. Very good weather. Watched the Olympics again. Went a walk to Tenby. An old lady asked us to help her get her husband back into bed but he was dead. Made her some tea. Doctor confirmed the death and gave us a lift home.

31 August 1972.

My diary entry:

Went to Amroth Beach and swam in the sea. Good weather. Mark Spitz won five gold medals for swimming at the Olympics and Kobut won the gymnastics (2 gold) very good. Had a barb-b-que on the beach sausage onions and drinks. Great fun.

We were having our family summer holiday in a Caravan Park in Saundersfoot, Pembrokeshire. Like all of our childhood summers, it was hot and sunny. My brother and I had made friends with Dave and Clare on the same site and we spent most of our days together like Enid Blyton children: outside, making adventures, as far away from adults as was possible.

We played games, went walking and swimming and made up stories when we were hidden in the overgrown brittle yellow grass. On this day we went a long hot walk along the coastal path, on the cliff tops, through the bracken and avoiding the stinging nettles, until we came to what we thought was an olde worlde village of cottages that faced into a lane. At one of the sun blistered doors there was an old lady, wearing a pinafore. Her face was like a walnut. She looked distressed. She waved us over towards her with a brown thin arm. Being the eldest of us all by a few months I asked, 'Hello. Can we help?'

She said, 'He's fallen out of bed. I need help to get my husband back into bed. He's old. He's not been well.'

We agreed to help.

The friend, who is named David and the second eldest and I went into the musty, quite dark cottage. I asked my brother and our other friend Clare to go and put the kettle on. David and I went up the winding wooden staircase. I could smell a smell. I didn't know what it was, but instinctively I did know. It was sweet like lily of the valley soap. I can never forget that.

In the bedroom, there is a bed covered in a pretty quilt, a dressing table and a dark wooden wardrobe. Beside the bed and the wall on the far side from the door is a man in blue and white striped pyjamas lying on the floor in an awkward shape. He's a bit crab like and so very still. His unshaven jaw is locked. His eyes are closed. His hands and feet are cold. The centre of his chest is a bit warm. I know this because I touch him. I know he is dead but the adventure story where you find a body in mysterious circumstances demands that you check thoroughly. David hands me the silver backed hand mirror from the dressing table to put against his mouth to check for breath. There is no cloud on the surface. I take his pulse. There is nothing.

I think David and I were so deep in shock that we had no shock. We were scientists.

I didn't want to leave the man on the floor because I felt sorry for him, so David and I lifted him onto the bed and covered him with a sheet. My brother clunked up the stairs to see what we were doing, and I hissed at him to get out of the room. 'Is he dead?'

'Probably. Go away.'

Downstairs in the sitting room amongst the best porcelain on the dresser and antimacassars, the old lady was sitting in her armchair. I rifled through the kitchen cupboards looking for brandy which I knew she would have for medicinal purposes and then I liberally spiked her cup of tea with it and put in extra sugar. She had a few sips. I held her mottled hand and said as gently as I could that I was sorry, but her husband was dead. She cried, 'No.' It was chilling.

I asked if she had a phone but she said the Big House in the village had the phone. We ran down the lane to a house that had tall black iron gates and pressed frantically on a bell. A middle-aged woman answered and came to the gate as we garbled our message about the old lady and her husband. She said she would call a doctor. We ran back.

A young doctor arrived. He looked at the four of us who had tried to be kind and do the right thing. He cared for the old lady whose life companion had died and he checked upstairs while we sat on the front doorstep in the late afternoon glow and waited. He arranged things. Then he took us back in his car to the caravan site. He explained that he had a lot to do now, but that the following evening he would come back, talk to our parents and take us for a bar-b-que on the beach.

My brother and I were late for tea and our excuse was disbelieved. 'Another one of your stories.' But the next evening the doctor was true to his word and made us out to be heroes of the hour to our parents. He rewarded us with baked potatoes in the ashes and spitting sausages from the flames. I think that was the nicest way for us to talk about the incident. We were sixteen, fifteen, fourteen and thirteen at the time, and we danced on the sand.

Fire starter again

Diary entry Sunday 25 May 1975

I fell asleep later on, and when I woke up there was a lot of putrid smelling smoke in the room and the curtains had caught fire from the joss stick. I tried to put it out with water from the wash basin but all I soaked were the books on the desk and my record player. The curtains continued to burn very quickly and hotly. I grabbed one end of the curtains and after shouting 'Fire' and a variety of swear words got the curtain into the corridor to have Kevin spray it from the hose.

I was really shocked and nervous but only my notes and curtains were damaged. Quite a drama. Went to see Sting at the Union to take my mind off what happened. I worked out the ending. I must have seen it on the cinema or somewhere.

Rikki came back and I told her about the fire etc. She didn't yell at me which I was expecting.

In my first year at university, I was in a hall of residence. It was a coach journey from the Uni. It was considered quite modern: low rise with single study bedrooms with a wash basin (not an en suite, that would have been luxury), so shared facilities, a dining room that catered for us, mixed, but no visitors overnight, officially, and a quadrangle garden which was neat and tidy. In the summer we used it for afternoon parties.

I was on the ground floor overlooking the garden. My friends Rikki, Jacki, Maggie, Janet, Kath, Cath were all on the same floor. We were quite a posse.

It was two weeks from the end of year finals: a warm late Sunday afternoon and I had been revising English and was feeling sleepy. I had been out late on the Saturday night for wine and pizza in that order.

I lit a joss stick and dozed off. The window was open a bit and the breeze wafted the curtain which caught on the joss stick and caught alight.

I was rudely awakened by loud and insistent banging on my door and shouts of 'Fire'. I opened the door groggily to find a boy I didn't know from upstairs, holding the end of the fire hose which he directed at my feet because the end of my long green dress was smouldering. Then he directed the hose at the brown curtains and some of the papers on the desk which were on fire. He drenched everything just to be certain that the fire was out.

He destroyed my library of books and essays with the spray foam. But to his credit he did save me for which I will be eternally grateful.

That fire nearly cost me my place at Uni. Never mind so called 'fire retardant' curtains: I had caused damage and although threatened with having to pay damages, the real damage was to my chance of reading English in Part Two. My notes and revision books were soaked or burnt. Everything stank of sooty embers. Luckily, kind friends, Janet and Maggie, let me borrow their work to copy up and I went on without flames for a few more years.

Which is true? My Diary or my memory? Or are both true in their own way?

And then Fire

I gave up smoking for good around 1998. My son of five, nagged and nagged and I told him I did it for him. Not quite true. I did it for me because I had too many bouts of bronchitis. So, this event happened in 1997 when I was still a heavy smoker.

I was a responsible senior leader in a large comprehensive school in a building not unlike my old hall of residence. My office was about the size of my old bedroom, minus the sink, and looked over a small quadrangle which was glass sided. It was a great position to be, on a corner, light and airy, and opposite the classroom where I taught seven hours a week. The downside was the smelly boys' toilet on the corridor opposite, but perhaps you can't have everything.

In those days, we were allowed to smoke in our offices, and I made full use of the privilege. At five minutes to the bell, I was rounding off some administration: I wrote the school timetable. I stubbed out my cigarette; emptied the ashtray into the bin and went to wash my hands quickly and chew some gum with the strongest mint flavour, before facing a class of thirty-two thirteen- and fourteen-year-old students, hoping I didn't reek of smoke. I always did.

The door to my classroom had a long glass panel with a direct line of sight across the quadrangle to my office. About ten minutes into the lesson, Tina said, 'Look, Miss, there's some smoke.'

'Where?'

'I think your office is on fire, Miss.'

'Is it?'

'Shouldn't you ring the alarm, Miss. Shouldn't we all go out?'

'No, I think it'll be OK.' I replied. I saw Andy from the office opposite to mine, with the fire extinguisher tackling the burning bin and my burning coat which hung above it. The air was misty blue and smelt of singed damp fabric.

'Burnt toast, I think,' I told the kids at the end of the poetry lesson. 'Off you go.'

Poetic license?

1999.

It was my turn to be on late duty at school. We ran clubs to five o'clock for homework, use of the library books and computers and extra curricula activities: swimming, team games, art and science club. There were frequently a hundred or so students dotted around the building on the ground floor with a teacher and more outside.

From my office I smelt smoke. Sometimes Emma, one of the Science teachers demonstrated various theses by burning pieces of bread, but this was acrid. I went along the long corridor towards the labs and was met by billowing smoke roiling down the stairs from one of the towers. This was a group of three upstairs classrooms with no corridor. They were above the photocopier and reprographics area which was full of chemicals.

It takes a lot to faze me. This was very serious. I pressed the fire alarm; called Andy the other manager on site on his mobile and started to run around the building banging on doors and shouting to get out, it wasn't a drill. Andy was running the other way round. I remember the response was pretty lackadaisical.

The fire brigade arrived. Blue lights. Lots of noise. Big men in highly bulked up clothing. Masks. White hoses. The students and teachers were all gathered outside on the car park to the front of the building while from behind it thick black smoke and tall flames were stretching out into the evening sky. The smoke belched over our heads. It became an inferno as the wooden furniture, books, paper and partition floors and walls caught alight. More fire engines arrived, and more hoses were deployed by fire fighters on tall ladders. Teachers and children, having seen the most exciting part, drifted off home. Andy and I had to stay because the local press wanted a statement. I was anodyne: no, no one had been hurt, no, I didn't know the cause of the fire. Yes, I had discovered it and called the fire brigade, no I wasn't the Headteacher.

The press called me a hero.

There were a few happy endings: the student who had set the fire was caught. The choking smell of smoke eventually left the atmosphere. The refurbishment of the tower area benefited us with a new space which we turned into a purpose-built Library for all and a few years later we won an award as Reading School of the Year.

I asked Emma to not do her burnt toast experiment for a while.

Out on the Red Sea. Day One

Day one, dive one.
Suit on, stretched and zipped
Tanks in place and 'regs' tested
Fins cumbersome
Mask lubricated.
'Ready?' Smiles of
encouragement.
My weights make my body
Arch awkwardly
As I waddle to the edge of the
Diving platform.
We are far out at sea.
Thumbs up. Silent pantomime.
Plunge.
The silence below the waves
Is immense.
The light filtering through
Dissolves from sugar white to
azure.
There is no horizon.
I look into the deep.
It is infinity.
Nothing but navy.
Liquid.
Like sky, like space
But here there is no midnight
star
Here there is only blue.
The first dive.
A Monday.

Breaking out

Breaking up
Breaking down
Breaking the speed limit
Breaking the law
Break dancing.
Breaking the record
Breaking point
Breaking bail
Breaking the ice
Coffee break.
Breaking and entering
Breaking news
Breaking the spell
Heart breaking.
Breaking the habit
Breaking camp
Breaking your neck
Even break.
Breaking cover
Breaking rank
Breaking the glass ceiling
Ground breaking.
Break a leg…

What did I do?   Broke my wrist.

Empty Nest

Illuminated by the lighted fridge
You eating all the cherry
tomatoes
Without apology
You leaving your cereal bowl
next
To the dishwasher
And your balled up socks
On the stairs
I miss that.
Your cargo jacket with the frayed
Cuffs hanging
on the hall stand
The creaking step at
One a.m.
Those bloody headphones
(for my benefit)
The open books on the couch
Tiny, tiny bits of whisker
You swear you rinsed away
I miss that.
Watching 'our' shows together
Another pizza nightEmpty
tomato packets in the fridge
Did I mention that?
I never thought I'd miss
The smell of your room
Standing bare footed on a
Rebel piece of Lego
Finding salted peanuts behind
the cushions
And chocolate wrappers under
The fridge
You denying liability
Me pretending I didn't know.
I never thought I could miss
Searching for one trainer
At 8.30 a.m.
Or arguing about putting it
back
Where it belongs.
Now I miss
Your untidiness
The quiet punctuated
By your key in the lock.
Your call,
'I'm back'…
I miss that.

Humidity

The nothing breeze
No wafting stalks
Brittle
Wrinkled leaves fallen
Rattled by footsteps.
Shadows darken
A spot of
A drop of
A spot of
A

Drop

Of

A

Spot

Of

Rain

                                        Relief.

For Jacki: who died March 2024

One might ask for:
Just ten more years to
Quaff the savvy blanc
Hug the grand kids
Cruise the Guernsey Coast
Hear his morning salutations.

Just five more years to
See the garden bloom
Pluck a grey eyebrow
Stroll to Antiques and Ales
Win at poker.

Just one more year to
Fall laughing in the snow
Have a birthday bash
Eat a sickly creme egg.

Just one more time:
Decorate the room
Control the light
Hit the heights.

To Gerard

For all you're able to do: thank you.
For all you can't do
Thank you for accepting that.
For all you want to do
Thank you for realising that.
For what tomorrow might bring-
For embracing that.
For your unity, thank you for that.
And when there is silence
Might you understand that.

To make an apple crumble

Take a comfortable spade.
Dig deep into rich dark dirt
Position two apple trees
Back fill and surround with
Three kilos of mixed mulch.
Fill the green watering can
Three times and water in.
Wait.

In the dry season
Add more water.
Wait.
Remove the spurs and gently
Prune.
Wait.

Pick off the crowding fruit
Let the tree breathe
Let the fruit swell.
Wait.

Pick. Peel. Core. Slice.
Simmer.
Layer apples and crumb
Bake.
Eat.
Pick. Peel. Core. Slice.
Simmer.
Layer apples and crumb
Bake.
Eat.

Three years to fruiting.
Will serve for fifty.

Garden: New Amsterdam. Surinam

Think of green.
Think of all the words
you know for green.
Think of short grass today that
tomorrow will be bold.
Think of trees that flash
with vermilion breasts
and custard yellow beaks.
Think of savage
aloe veras sucking the sand
to friable tracks.
Think of brittle palms
rattling in the scorched air -
fronds grey -green -gold
chaffing at the fruit
Think.

From across the forest heights
of rosewood, kapok, mahogany,
the swooping storm
soaks green.

Marooned

They were upstairs now. Their front bedroom looked like a store room with brown boxes stacked against the walls leaving only narrow walk ways between the sides of the bed and the wardrobe and door. They could lie on the bed and see words in every language patterning the cardboard. The other bedrooms fared no better. Legs of chairs spiked the air; black plastic bags holding mysterious shapes were bundled on top of three storey chests of drawers and bright red and green plastic storage boxes from the Pound Shop. Nothing was labelled.

From the bathroom he could hear her singing, 'Row, row, row your boat across the kitchen floor. Merrily, merrily, merrily, who could ask for more?'

It was one of the children's favourite tunes from a very old television programme. He made himself remember. Mice in a pink ballet shoe. He smiled. That was it, mice rowing a ballet shoe around the house and down the stairs. Funny how those things pop into your head. He heard his wife come out of the bathroom, still humming. She came and sat on the bed.

'You know, one of my happiest times was when we were first married,' she said with a smile that creased her whole face, 'and you used to read to me. I can remember about three books that we read out loud to each other, but my favourite was that one about messing about in a boat.'

'Jerome K. Jerome,' he said. 'They've made a programme about it now. Probably the BBC. It's the sort of whimsy-thing they like to do, isn't it? Sunlight on the water and rather nice period costumes and sparkling dialogue.' He said it without bitterness. 'I doubt we'll be able to see it now.'

'Well, you read it rather exquisitely, and I should very much like to have you read it to me again sometime.' She patted his arm. Her voice was full of fondness. 'Not sure where we put all the books, are you?' She looked around the room vaguely. 'We did bring them up, didn't we?'

He stretched out on the bed and laced his gnarled hands behind his head. 'Oh yes. They're here somewhere and I will look for them the next time I go foraging. You know, I could do with a sandwich. Shame I can't toast it.' He carefully swung his slippered feet over the side of the bed and stood up with a little noise. 'Would you like something, dear?'

'What? Oh no...no. I'm fine, thank you. I'll wait till later. My pills though. I need those. And a bottle of water please. The taps are not working. I'll take my pills and then I suppose...' He had disappeared into the makeshift kitchenette and didn't hear the rest.

He returned munching bread and butter. 'You know,' he said between mouthfuls, 'It's going to cost a lot to get the car fixed up. It'll be the catalytic converter that will cause the problem. The moisture will have got into it.'

'Isn't it still under warranty?' She took the small bottle of water from him.

'Yes, but even if that covers it and the insurance we'll have to pay the excess at least and that will be a tidy sum. We did bring all the papers for it, right? I'll phone them up later and see what they say. We've still got the mobile. Has it got a charge left on it?'

'I think we should wait. We might need it for something more pressing. We'll not be using the car for a while. Let's save the battery for now.' She slipped the phone into her pocket. 'You know,' she mused, 'we haven't had a holiday for ages. We should go to Venice again. I rather liked that bridge and the photograph you took of me there. I know you cut the top of my head off in the picture but we could go back and redo it.' She smiled hopefully.

'I did not cut your head off! You moved!' He laughed. Now we've got that fancy mobile cutting heads off is a thing of the past. Just do it again. No waiting for a packet from Boots and laughing and crying over bad shots and sorting ones for the albums. You did pack those?'

Yes, don't fret. They're here somewhere.'

'Yes, Venice is very lovely. We should go again while we still can. And Pompeii. Those are cities that have had their ups and downs. What with one form of destruction and another, and now threatened again. What's left? You can't fathom it, can you?'

'It's inertia. No one wants to take responsibility for anything.'

'Oh sorry. Why does it always land butter side down? Now it'll mark the duvet cover. A bit like when we were students eh? Crumbs in the bed...'

'I remember yours being a bit worse than that!' She sipped from the bottle. 'You know the other day, after that first alert, I saw some people in a car just staring into the ford and watching the water. Doing nothing. Total inertia. Not helping themselves at all. You were already packing up stuff. I wonder if they just floated away...'

There was a loud gurgle and sucking noise from the staircase.

'Sounds like the tide has turned,' he said, 'in a manner of speaking.'

'Time and tide wait for no man,' she chipped in. 'Water, water everywhere and...'

'Only a bottle to drink. I might try a wade downstairs to get something for later. A bottle of claret do you?'

'That would be lovely. But you must be careful.'

'Of course. We've still got that antibac stuff haven't we? And I'll bring more buckets if I can. They'll be useful.'

With his fishing waders strapped on carefully, he stepped gingerly from the step into the foul smelling, brown sticky water. He actions were a little clumsy and he held the bannister tightly.

The downstairs of the house looked alien and distorted. A kettle floated off the range. Through the sitting room window he could see the sunlight dappling on the water as it lapped over the window sill.

'More than a catalytic converter,' he thought.

Two Beds

In Whitstable
My bed is wide and
white linens
are tight,
satin smooth.
The base: firm and deep
no sags or creaky springs.
I am compressed and
cool.
I can spread eagle,
turn, wrestle the covers,
find a cold edge
to chill on,
or a warm wrap.

In Surinam
Your bed has lumps.
Under your pillow
a clunky Glock.
Strapped to the frame
a sheathed, curved
bone handled blade.

Above our heads a
micronet,
but in my ear
a buzz.
Across my chest
a slick of sweat.

The air is all heat.

I lie blinking
in time to the numbers
changing on the clock,
notice the silence of the frogs
before the roar of the rain.

Acknowledgments

This anthology would not have been possible without the Creative Writing Group in Canterbury whose unwavering support I salute. Cheers to Emma, Becki, Debbie, Emily and Nick.